# A BOY Had a MOTHER Who Bought HIM a HAT

By KARLA KUSKIN

Illustrated by KEVIN HAWKES

**HARPER**
*An Imprint of HarperCollinsPublishers*

A boy had a mother who bought him a hat,
red as a rose
and it kept off the snows.

He loved it so much
that whatever he did
or whatever he said
he wore his new hat
which was woolly and red.

He stood in a wood
in his hat,
on his head.

So then she went out and she bought him a mouse.
Sniffing and squeaking
and seeking and peeking.

He loved it so much
that whatever he did
or whatever he said
when dressed in his hat
which was woolly and red,
he included his mouse,

and he built it a small
very comfortable house
which he painted sky blue.
He went to a party.
The mouse went there too.

Well then she went out and she bought him new shoes,
brown ones with laces for going to places.

He loved them so much
that whatever he did
or whatever he said
when dressed in his hat
which was woolly and red,
while holding his mouse
in its house of sky blue
he wore his two shoes
which were shiny and new.

They looked very dashing
and dapper on him
when he walked to the seashore
and went for a swim.

After that she went out and she bought him new boots,
a black rubber pair like the firemen wear.

He loved them so much
that whatever he did
or whatever he said
when dressed in his hat
which was woolly and red,
while holding his mouse
in its house of sky blue,
and wearing his shoes
which were hidden
but new,
he did with his boots on.

No reason to laugh
except that he wore them
while taking a bath.

The next day she bought him some very nice skis,
waxed to a glow to cut tracks through the snow.

He loved them so much
that whatever he did
or whatever he said
when dressed in his hat
which was woolly and red,
while holding his mouse
in its house of sky blue,
and wearing his shoes
which were shiny and new
hidden under his boots
which were very new too
he did with his skis on,

and though a beginner
he wore them one night
to his Grandma's for dinner.

On Halloween evening she bought him a mask.
It made him quite merry to look very scary.

He loved it so much
that whatever he did
or whatever he said
when dressed in his hat
which was woolly and red,
while holding his mouse
in its house of sky blue,
and wearing his shoes
which were shiny and new,

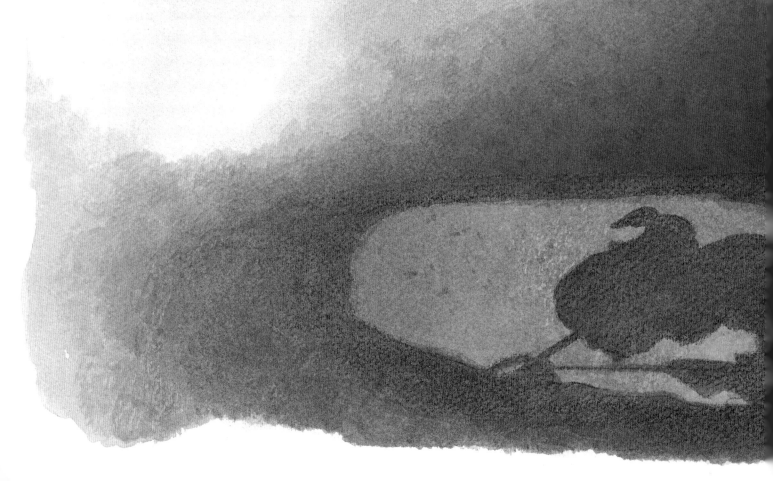

hidden under his boots
which were very new too,
well strapped to his skis
which were yellow and bright,

from dawn until dusk
until noon until night,
he kept on his mask
and looked ghostly or worse.
When he went to the doctor's
he frightened the nurse.

She went out one day and she bought him a cello.
You know you don't blow it.
To play it you bow it.

He loved it so much
that whatever he did
or whatever he said
when dressed in his hat
which was woolly and red,
while holding his mouse
in its house of sky blue,
and wearing his shoes
which were shiny and new,
hidden under his boots
which were pretty new too,
well strapped to his skis
which were polished and bright,
from dawn until dusk
until noon until night
with his Halloween mask
(very scary and yellow)
he NEVER let go
of his elegant cello.

He played away worry
and hurry and care;
he played for some rabbits,
five birds and a bear.

She went out once more and she bought him an elephant.
But not just a small one—a heavy, grey, tall one.

He loved it so much
that whatever he did
or whatever he said
when dressed in his hat
which was woolly and red,
while holding his mouse
in its house of sky blue,
and wearing his shoes
which were shiny and new,
hidden under his boots
which looked almost new too,
well strapped to his skis
which were polished and bright,
from dawn until dusk
until noon until night
with his Halloween mask
which was scary and yellow,
from summer through winter
embracing his cello,

his elephant went
and they raced everywhere

until in a frost frozen flurry of air
his hat blew away
and it left his hair bare
to the wild windy roar.

Then his mother yelled,
"Dear, I am off to the store.
It is very clear that
you must have a new hat."
And she rushed out the door.

*For Swanee, who is also Ian*
*—K.K.*

*To Lori and Anton, who have given Nathaniel many hats*
*—K.H.*

A Boy Had a Mother Who Bought Him a Hat
Text copyright © 1976 by Karla Kuskin
Illustrations copyright © 2010 by Kevin Hawkes

Manufactured in China.
Library of Congress Cataloging-in-Publication Data
Kuskin, Karla.
    A boy had a mother who bought him a hat / by Karla Kuskin ; illustrated by Kevin Hawkes. — 1st ed.
       p.     cm.
    Summary: After a boy's mother buys him a hat, she buys him a mouse, shoes, boots, skis, mask, cello, and an elephant—none
of which he is ever without.
    ISBN 978-0-06-075330-6 (trade bdg.) — ISBN 978-0-06-075331-3 (lib. bdg.)
    [1. Mother and child—Fiction.   2. Stories in rhyme.]  I. Hawkes, Kevin, ill  II. Title.
PZ8.3.K96Bo   2010                                               2006100114
[E]—dc22                                                      CIP
                                                                          AC

Typography by Jennifer Rozbruch
10  11  12  13    SCP    10  9  8  7  6  5  4  3
❖
First Edition